Diggy's Discovery Day

By: Zaedyn Williams

"Rise and shine, Diggy! Better go ahead and get dressed so you can make it to school in time for breakfast."

Diggy jumps out of bed full of energy
and his excited to start his day.

"You got it, Mom! I hope they have my favorite today. You know, bacon, eggs and toast?"

"Diggy, did you remember to grab your homework?"

"No, I actually forgot. But, I will let my teacher know that I'll have it first thing tomorrow."

SCHOOL

"Diggy, you have to do better at keeping up with your assignments and classwork or you'll get behind.", says his mom.

"I know. Sometimes, it just feels like my brain is moving so fast I can't keep all my thoughts straight."

Diggy rushes out the car.

SCHOOL

"This line is too long.
I'm just going to skip everyone.
They won't mind, I'm a growing boy."

Ms. Joy begins to speak. "Okay class,
What's the answer to..."

Diggy while wiggling in his seat, interrupts without
raising his hand or waiting
for the teacher to finish the question.

Class is dismissed. Diggy is embarrassed.
His teacher picks up the phone to call his mom.

"Hi Ms. Dragon. I wanted to share Diggy's behavior today with you."

Mommy Dragon responds. "Not again... Well, he has been really hyper. It's been hard for him to pay attention to things and he's seemed jumpy for the last 6 months in more than one setting."

"Have you thought about having him evaluated for ADHD?", ask Ms. Joy.

12
9
3
6
1 2 3 5 8 13 21 34 55 89 144 233 377 610 987
4 may, Monday
Maths

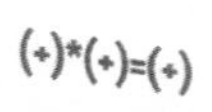
(+)*(+)=(+)
(-)*(-)=(+)
(-)*(+)=(-)
(+)*(-)=(-)
$x^a \cdot x^b = x^{a+b}$ $(x^a)^b = x^{a \cdot b}$
$x^a : x^b = x^{a-b}$ $1/x^a = x^{-a}$

"Ms. Joy called me. She told me you
blurted out answers in class, skipped lines,
and forgot your homework.
I've noticed these things for a while at home too,
but I thought it was something you'd grow out of.
Just to make sure you are getting all the
support and resources you need to thrive,
we are going to see our doctor friend, Dr. Onya."

"I've completed my evaluation of Diggy;
he is perfectly fine. He just has
attention-deficit/hyperactivity disorder.
It's called ADHD for short. This is why he has had
some many struggles with impulsivity like being jumpy,
hyperactivity, and inattentiveness where
it's hard for him to focus. By offering
him accommodations and modifications to
his daily life, we can
help him thrive.", says Dr. Onya.

Dr. Onya

"I'm so happy we saw Dr. Onya and
were able find out how we could help you best."

"Me too. I feel like we unlocked all of my superpowers.", says Diggy.
Diggy and Mom high five.

Made in the USA
Las Vegas, NV
24 May 2021